BUZBY

THE MISBEHAVING BEE

Also Available

Board Books:
Buzby the Misbehaving Bee
Flo the Lyin' Fly
Flood of Lies
Hermie and the Big Bully Croaker
Hermie: A Common Caterpillar
Rock, Roll, and Run
Stuck in a Stinky Den
The Caterpillars of Ha-Ha
The 12 Bugs of Christmas
Webster the Scaredy Spider

Picture Books:
Hermie: A Common Caterpillar
Flo the Lyin' Fly
The 12 Bugs of Christmas (includes DVD)
Webster the Scaredy Spider

Buginnings Series:
ABCs
Colors
Numbers
Shapes

Journal:
My First Prayer Journal

Holy Bible:
Max Lucado's Hermie & Friends™ Bible

Videos & DVDs:
Buzby the Misbehaving Bee
Hermie: A Common Caterpillar
Flo the Lyin' Fly
Webster the Scaredy Spider

MAX LUCADO'S
HeRMIe & Friends™

BUZBY
THE MISBEHAVING BEE

Story by Troy Schmidt
Illustrations by GlueWorks Animation
Based on the characters from Max Lucado's
Hermie: A Common Caterpillar

www.tommynelson.com
A Division of Thomas Nelson, Inc.
www.ThomasNelson.com

Published in Nashville, Tennessee, by Tommy Nelson®, a Division of Thomas Nelson, Inc.
Tommy Nelson® books may be purchased in bulk for educational, business, fund-raising, or sales promotional use. For information, please email SpecialMarkets@ThomasNelson.com.

Scripture quotations in this book are from the International Children's Bible®, New Century Version®, © 1986, 1988, 1999 by Tommy Nelson®, a Division of Thomas Nelson, Inc. All rights reserved.

Library of Congress Cataloging-in-Publication Data

Schmidt, Troy.
   Buzby the misbehaving bee/story by Troy Schmidt; illustrations by GlueWorks Animation.
      p. cm.—(Max Lucado's Hermie & friends)
   "Based on the characters from Max Lucado's *Hermie: A Common Caterpillar*."
   Summary: Buzby thinks he is too cool for rules, and ladybug twins Hailey and Bailey admire him for it, until he lets a huge frog into the garden, putting everyone at risk, and finally must ask God for forgiveness and help.
   ISBN 1-4003-0510-1 (hardback)
   [1. Behavior—Fiction. 2. Rules (Philosophy)—Fiction. 3. Conduct of life—Fiction. 4. Bees—Fiction.
5. Insects—Fiction. 6. Frogs—Fiction.] I. GlueWorks Animation. II. Title. III. Series.
PZ7.S3565Bu 2005
[E]—dc22

2004020827

Printed in the United States of America

05 06 07 08 09 PHX 5 4 3 2 1

www.hermieandfriends.com
Email us at: comments@hermieandfriends.com

"Remember my laws and rules, and obey them.
Then you will live safely in the land."
—Leviticus 25:18

Buzby the misbehaving bee never followed the rules. Finally, the other bees told him, "Don't come back until you learn to follow the rules!"

Buzby didn't care. "I'm too cool for rules," Buzby said. "I'll start my own beehive, and I'll be *king* of the bees."

That night, Buzby started building his new hive. All the loud hammering and sawing noises woke up Hermie the caterpillar.

Buzby didn't care. "I'm too cool for rules," Buzby said. "I'm *king* of the bees, and I'll do as I please."

And he did.

But the noise kept Hermie awake all night.

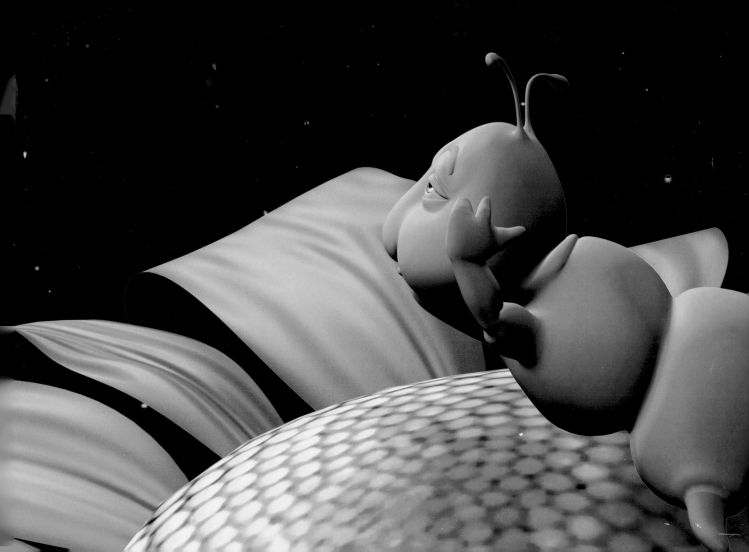

The next morning, Hermie agreed to watch Lucy Ladybug's twins, Hailey and Bailey. Just as the ladybugs arrived, Buzby buzzed by so fast that it turned Hermie, Wormie, and Lucy upside down! The twins laughed.

"Who is that?" Hailey asked.

"He's soooo cool." Bailey sighed.

"That's Buzby," Hermie said. "He *thinks* he's king of the bees."

Before she left, Lucy reminded the twins of the rules: "Stay with Hermie, and do as he says."

"Yes, Mama," the twins said.

But Hailey and Bailey didn't obey the rules.

While Hermie and Wormie were talking, the twins sneaked away to find Buzby.

When Hermie and Wormie realized the twins were gone, they started looking for them.

Hermie and Wormie found Hailey
and Bailey watching Buzby at his new beehive.

"This place is a mess," Wormie whispered to Hermie.

"Buzby, let us show you the Garden Golden Rules,"
Hermie said.

"Rules? I'm too cool for rules," Buzby said. "I'm *king*
of the bees, and I'll do as I please."

"Yes, I know," said Hermie. "But follow me anyway."

"Well . . . okay," Buzby said.

THE GARDEN
GOLDEN RULES

1. Always listen to God.

2. Don't open the gate!

3. Do listen to your parents.

4. Do help one another.

5. Do love one another.

6. Don't hurt another bug's feelings.

7. Don't make a mess.

8. Don't cause others to do wrong.

9. No speeding.

10. No loud noises after bedtime.

The group went to the rock with the Garden Golden Rules written on it. Hermie read the rules out loud.

Buzby shook his head. "I'm too cool for rules,"
Buzby said. "I'm *king* of the bees, and I'll do
as I please." And he left.

"I think he's trouble," said Hermie.

"Yes," Wormie agreed.

"I think he's cool," said Hailey.

"He's supercool," Bailey agreed.

Buzby broke all of the Garden Golden Rules.
He even dropped acorns on the ants' hill.

And all the while, Buzby said: "I'm too cool for
rules! I'm *king* of the bees, and I'll do as I please."

And he did.

Lucy Ladybug told her twins, "Stay away from that
misbehaving Buzby." But the twins didn't listen.

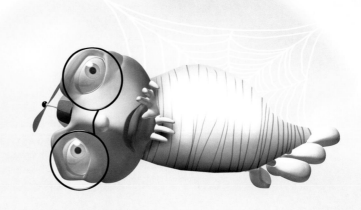

Hermie and Wormie prayed to God for help with Buzby.

God knew about Buzby. "I've known many like Buzby who don't like to follow the rules. Buzby doesn't understand that rules are to keep him and others safe. Rules are a way of saying, 'I love you.'"

God promised He would talk to Buzby.

Buzby took a sip of honey and smacked his lips.
"I'm *king* of the bees. That's me."

Then he heard a voice call his name.

"Buzby."

"Who said that?" Buzby looked around.
"Who is talking to the king of the bees?"

"It's God, Buzby. I'm the *King of Everything*.
You should follow the Garden Golden Rules."

Buzby didn't want to listen to God. He flew away.

Later, Buzby met Hailey and Bailey at the big fence gate. "Let's open it," Buzby said.

The twins stepped back. "We're not supposed to open the gate, and that's a rule we'd better follow," Hailey said.

"I'm too cool for rules!" Buzby said. "I'm *king* of the bees, and I'll do as I please. Watch me!"

Slowly, Buzby opened the gate.

DO NOT OPEN

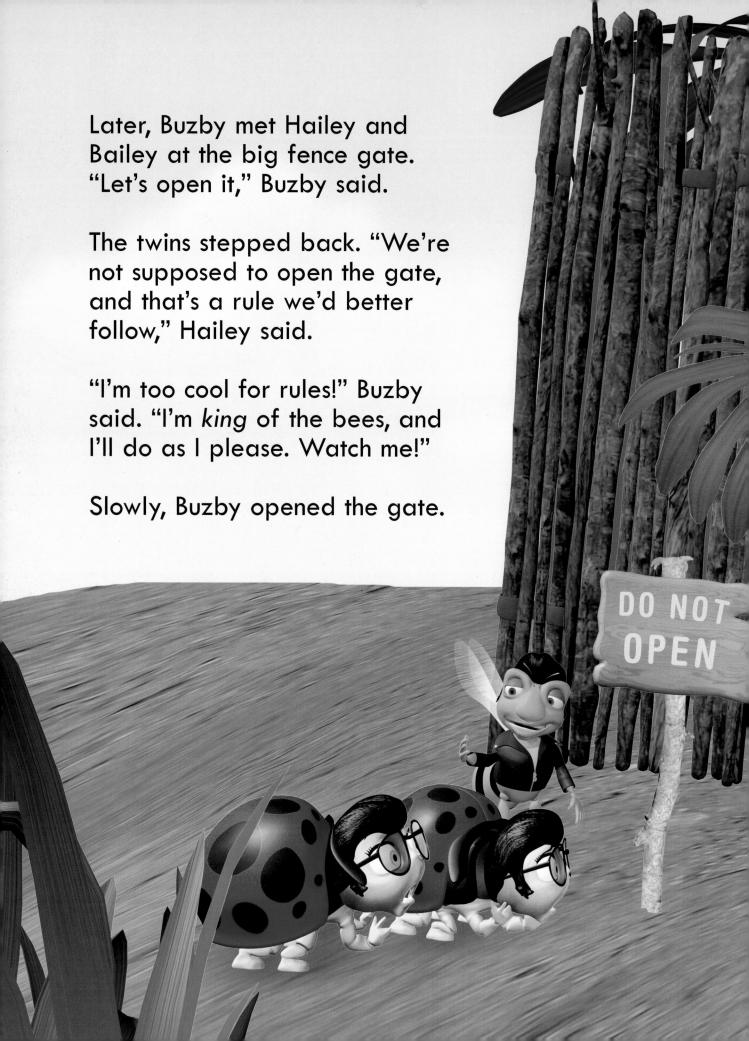

First there was silence. Then a rumbling.
Then a shaking. Then a quaking.

Then, standing before Buzby, Hailey, and
Bailey was a BIG frog.

"Big Bully Croaker!" Hailey screamed.

"Run for your life!" Bailey shouted.

"Uh-oh. Big frog. Not cool." Buzby
ran away, too.

The BIG frog hopped through the garden, smashing everything in his path. He hopped so high, he even knocked Buzby's beehive to the ground.

"Oh, no! My beehive is broken. The king of the bees has no home." Buzby was sad.

"Buzby," God said.

Buzby still didn't want to listen to God. Buzby flew away.

The ants found Buzby's broken hive and put it back together.

"This hive belongs to the bee who dropped acorns on our hill," Art Ant said.

"That doesn't matter. We're doing what would please God," Antonio Ant said.

Meanwhile, other garden bugs had 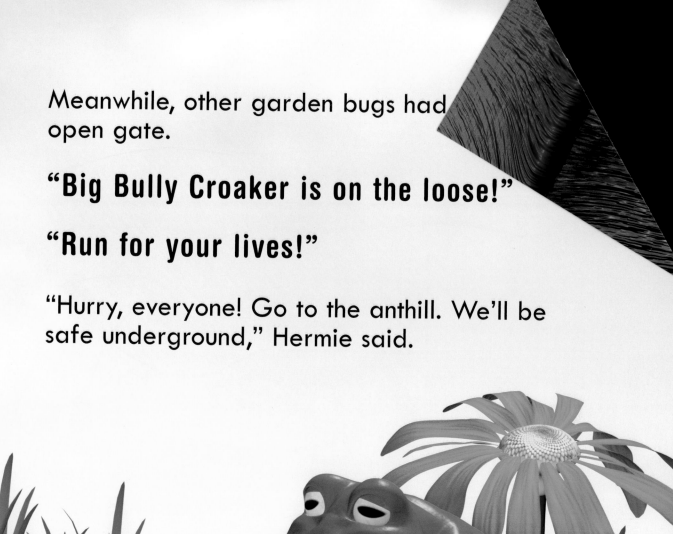 open gate.

"Big Bully Croaker is on the loose!"

"Run for your lives!"

"Hurry, everyone! Go to the anthill. We'll be safe underground," Hermie said.

Buzby found a new place to live. He didn't know it was Flo the fly's home.

Just then Buzby heard a voice call his name.

"Oh, no!" Buzby said. "It's God!" Buzby *still* didn't want to listen to God. Buzby quickly flew away.

At the anthill, the garden friends were all jumping into the ants' home to hide. Just as the last one made it safely inside, they heard . . .

THUMP!

Big Bully Croaker had plopped down on the door to the anthill. Everyone inside was TRAPPED!

"Who let the frog out?" asked Antonio Ant.

Bailey Ladybug blurted out, **"Buzby did it!"**

"But we were with him," Hailey said.

Lucy was disappointed that the twins had
disobeyed her. "Rules are to keep you and
others from getting hurt," she said. "Look what
breaking one rule has done."

"We are very sorry we disobeyed," the twins said.
"We promise to follow the rules from now on."

When Buzby saw that the ants had fixed his hive, he felt bad about dropping acorns on their hill.

He prayed: "God, I'm sorry I broke the rules. I promise to obey them from now on. Will You forgive me?"

"Of course, Buzby," God said. "I love you. That's why I have rules to keep you safe."

Then God told Buzby to rescue the others. And this time Buzby listened.

Buzby flew toward the giant frog. Big Bully
Croaker tried to grab Buzby with his tongue.
Buzby pointed his stinger at the frog.

"Let my friends go!" Buzby said.

Now, bees don't like frogs, but frogs REALLY don't like angry bees.

Big Bully Croaker jumped off that anthill and quickly hopped away.

Everyone thanked Buzby for rescuing them. "Listen up," Buzby said. "I'm sorry I broke the garden rules. Now I know that rules are cool. Will you forgive me?"

And they did. Buzby's bee friends also forgave him.

God was happy with Buzby, too. From now on, Buzby would listen to God and follow the rules.